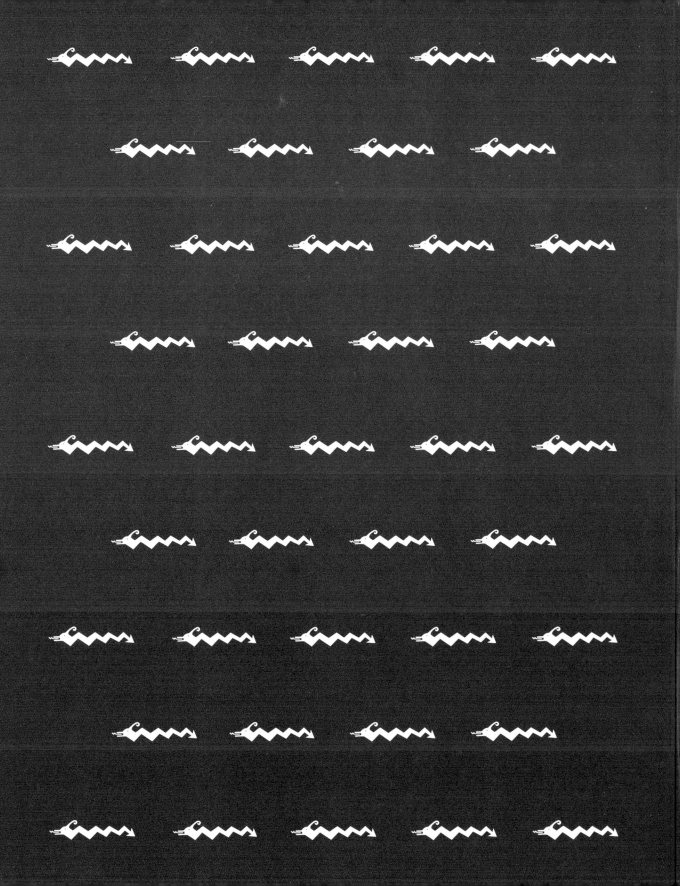

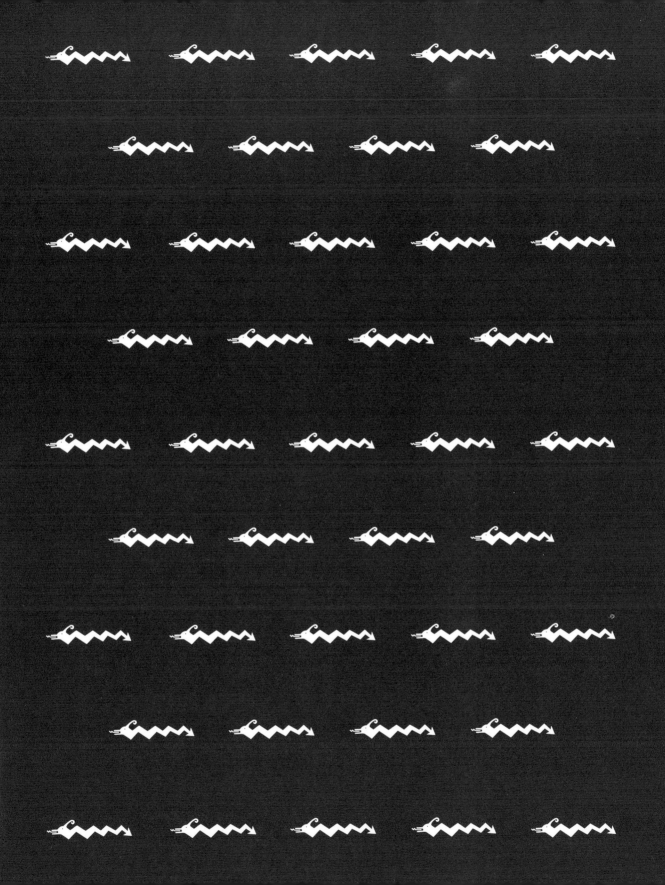

A First Clay
Gathering

by Nora Naranjo-Morse

Illustrated by
Roger Montoya

MULTICULTURAL CELEBRATIONS II

MODERN CURRICULUM PRESS

Multicultural Celebrations was created under the auspices of
 The Children's Museum, Boston.
Leslie Swartz, Director of Teacher Services,
directed this project.

Design: Gary Fujiwara
Photographs: *5*, Martin Rogers/TSW;
9, Palmer/Kane/TSW; *18*, Robert Frerck/TSW.

MODERN CURRICULUM PRESS, INC.
13900 Prospect Road
Cleveland, Ohio 44136

Published simultaneously in Canada by Globe/Modern Curriculum Press, Toronto.

ISBN 0-8136-2345-6 (soft cover)   0-8136-2346-4 (hard cover)

2 3 4 5 6 7 8 9 10   95 94

Simon & Schuster   A Paramount Communications Company

A bolt of lightning danced wildly across the sky. It crackled above the *adobe* homes of Kaa Povi and her family. The clay brick buildings looked dusty and ready for rain.

"Gia, will we still gather clay today, even with the rain?" Kaa Povi asked her mother.

"You will see, Kaa Povi. The June rain is just settling the dust," her mother said. "The mountain roads will be dry. This will be our first chance this year to gather clay. We must go —rain or no rain."

"Yes, today we must go," Kaa Povi said, watching her mother smooth a delicate clay bowl. On the shelf sat more traditional *Tewa*-style pots — smooth and strong and round. These pots her grandmother had made.

2

Always she had been a helper in clay gathering. Always she handed tools to her mother or brought water to her grandmother as they made their pottery. Always Kaa Povi had been fascinated by the shapes that grew out of dirt. Maybe she soon would add fine pots of her own to the shelf—pots of her own design.

She often dreamed of making bowls as beautiful as her mother's, and those of the other *Tewa* people. Always she had felt awkward working with the clay.

Always, as today, she asked herself, "When will the clay coil perfectly round for me like it does for Saa Yaa and the other people of our village?"

"Here comes your grandmother," her mother said looking up. "Saa Yaa, you're a little early. We can get going."

Kaa Povi greeted her grandmother. "*Senge taa muu*," she said. "I will put your clay buckets in the truck."

"Thank you, little one," Saa Yaa said as she climbed into the truck. "I move like a turtle, careful and slow!"

6

As her mother drove, Kaa Povi looked at the familiar scenes. For a long, long time, the *Tewa* have lived in *pueblos* along the Rio Grande in New Mexico. Kaa Povi's family lives in the Santa Clara *Pueblo*. It is near this pueblo that they would gather the clay to make their pottery. *Tewa* people had been doing this for almost 2,000 years.

"Gia, when did you know it was time to join the tradition of the clay?

"I guess I was ten— about your age, Kaa Povi," her mother answered, looking at her and smiling. "But, don't worry. The clay is already a part of who you are—a *Tewa*. You will know when you are ready to create."

As the truck climbed higher in the mountains, a furry-tailed red fox darted past. Saa Yaa pointed. "Look, our friend has led us to the clay road."

The sun's rays flashed brightly through the family of aspen trees. Kaa Povi's eyes grew wide.

"Saa Yaa, the road is like bright gold."

"In a way it is gold, Kaa Povi," Saa Yaa smiled as she spoke. "The clay we are looking for is here. It is very strong because it has tiny flecks of *mica* in it. This clay is a gift from Mother Earth."

"We made it," her mother said, stopping the truck.

"Remember," Saa Yaa said, "we come as guests of the mountains on this day to gather clay. We must be respectful of the earth."

Kaa Povi and Saa Yaa carried buckets to the clay pit. Almost without thinking, Kaa Povi walked right to the vein, the line in the pit with the purest clay. Saa Yaa began to laugh. "You must already know where the best spot is."

Kaa Povi watched as Saa Yaa carefully examined each handful of clay. "The clay is good—the very best. It will make bowls we can be proud of."

13

Kaa Povi smelled the moist, brown earth. She loosened some lumps of clay. As she picked them up, she knew, as grandmother had said, this clay was good.

Through the morning grandmother, mother and daughter dug with shovels and picks. They collected only the purest nuggets. Kaa Povi's hands seemed to know which nuggets to take. She sighed with relief when all the buckets were full and packed neatly in the truck bed.

Saa Yaa nodded her head. "This is enough. It is good that we take only what we need."

14

"As always, we will cover the clay pit with rocks and branches," her mother said.

Kaa Povi knew that if the pit was left uncovered it would be like a wound on Mother Earth's skin. Covering it would help it heal, and the clay would stay moist and ready for the next digging.

The sky turned gray. A cloudburst sprinkled raindrops on the three *Tewa* women as they finished their work. As quickly as it had come, it passed.

Kaa Povi looked up and gasped. Now the sky was a rainbow of color. It glowed all the way to the far horizon where it touched the land.

Suddenly, Kaa Povi's hands tingled with energy and excitement. Her arms caked with clay felt electric. From this clay, she knew would come round coils for pots. She knew it.

"It has been a good day. If I weren't so tired, I'd feel like celebrating... celebrating my connection with the clay," Kaa Povi said softly to herself.

18

Glossary

adobe (ah-DOH-bee) bricks made from clay that have been dried in the sun

mica (MI-kuh) a shiny, flakey mineral found in the earth

Pueblo (PWE-bloh) a member of one of the Native American groups of the Southwest

pueblo (PWE-bloh) the large buldings, like apartments, in which the Pueblo people live

Senge taa muu (SEN-jay-TAH-MOO) Tewa saying that means "welcome sun."

Tewa (TAY-wah) a member of one of the Pueblo groups; also the language of these people

About the Author

Nora Naranjo-Morse teaches the techniques of Santa Clara Pueblo pottery in her family, all over the United States, and in other countries. She has put her pottery on exhibit and published her poetry widely. In the Pueblo tradition, Nora, her daughter, and her mother still gather their own clay near their home in New Mexico.

About the Illustrator

Roger Montoya is an accomplished painter even though he never went to art school. A talented athlete, he became a professional dancer after graduating from college. In 1989, he decided to spend more time on his art, and has been painting ever since. This is the first children's book he has illustrated.

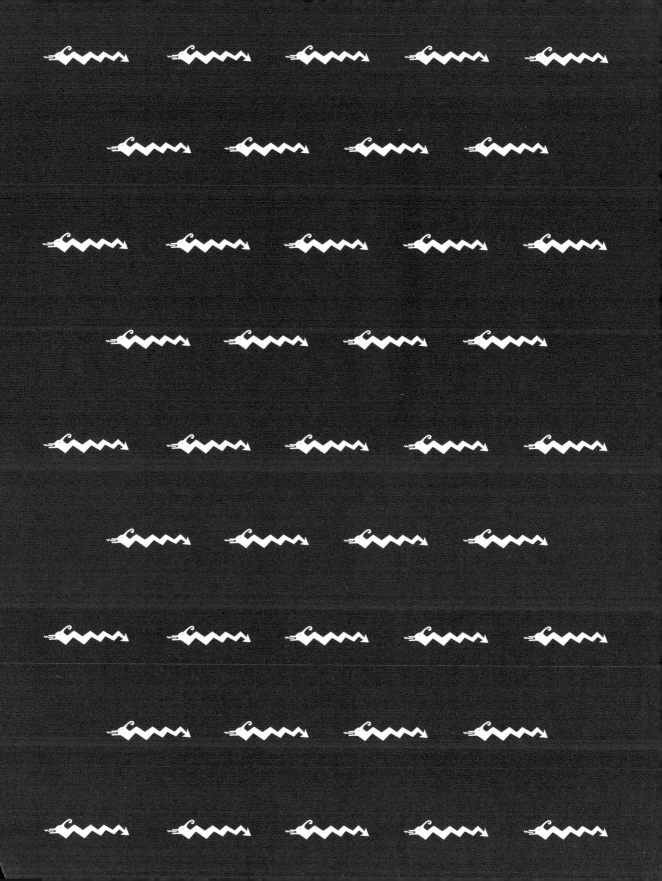

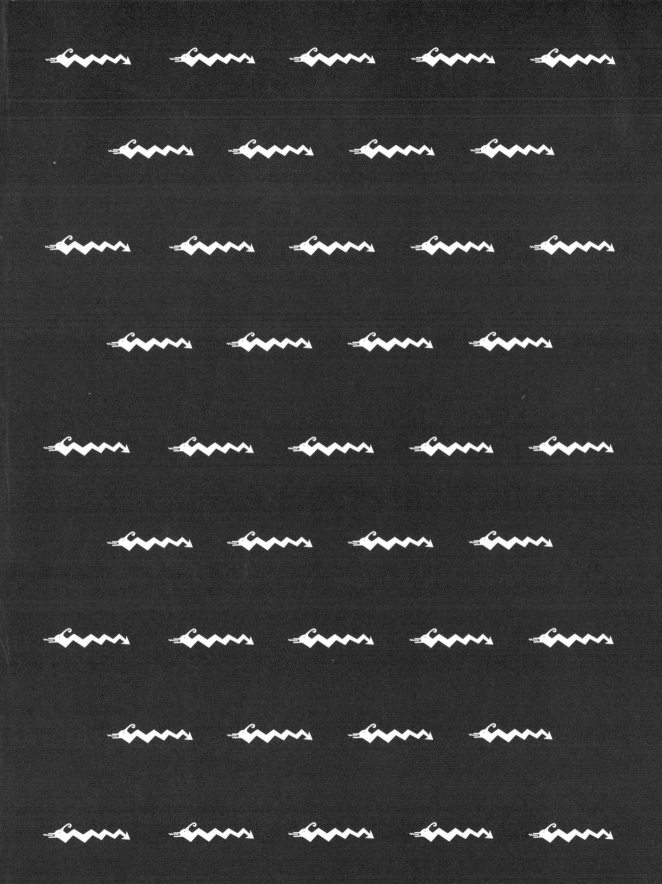